Spot's Baby Sister

Eric Hill

PUFFIN

Spot, we have a surprise for you!

It's your baby sister!

We have a present for you, Spot.

Who is at the door?

Spot looks for a toy for Susie.

What has Susie taken?

Where's Susie?

What's under the table,

Spot?

Time

for a nap, Susie.

Who's there?

You're a

big brother now, Spot!

I like Susie, Mum. She's fun!

PUFFIN BOOKS

Published by the Penguin Group: London, New York,
Australia, Canada, India, Ireland, New Zealand and South Africa
Penguin Books Ltd, Registered Offices:
80 Strand, London WC2R 0RL, England

puffinbooks.com

First published by William Heinemann Ltd, 1989
Published in Puffin Books 1991

27 29 30 28

Copyright © Eric Hill, 1989
All rights reserved

The moral right of the author/illustrator has been asserted

Printed and bound in Singapore

ISBN 978–0–140–54288–2